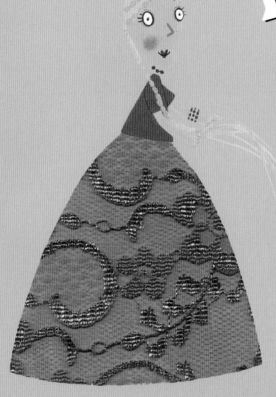

Falling
for
Rapunzel

G. P. PUTNAM'S SONS

Falling
for
Rapunzel

Leah Wilcox

illustrated by

Lydia Monks

Once upon a bad hair day,
a prince rode up Rapunzel's way.

From up above he heard her whine,
upset her hair had lost its shine.

He thought her crying was a plea
and sallied forth to set her free.

Alas, she was too far away
to quite make out what he would say:

"Rapunzel, Rapunzel, throw down your hair!"

She thought he said,
"Your underwear."

"No, Rapunzel.
Your curly locks!"

Rapunzel threw down dirty socks.

"Please, love, just your **silky tresses!**"
She thought he asked for silky dresses.

In lace and frills up to his head,
the prince's cheeks were blushing red.

"Rapunzel, do you have a **rope?**"

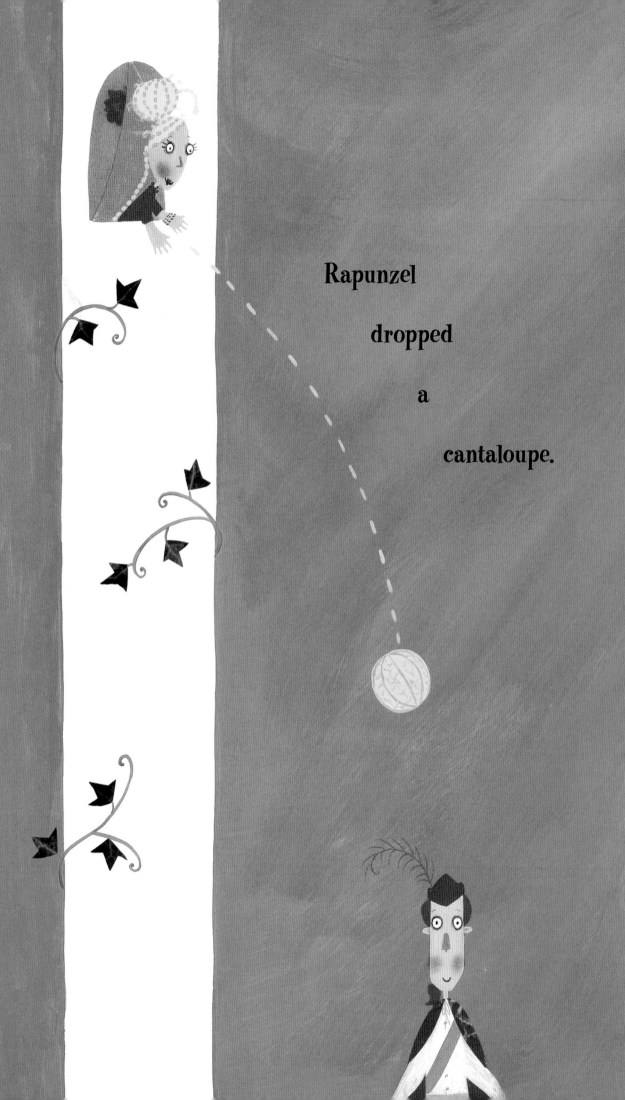

Rapunzel

dropped

a

cantaloupe.

It burst in pieces
on his head.
"Oh, bad catch!"
Rapunzel said.

"Perhaps," he sighed,
"this is a test."
And bound by love
he did not rest.

"O.K., Rapunzel, how 'bout **twine?**"

She

heaved

out

her

blue-ribbon

swine.

By now the prince was feeling hammered,
not to mention less enamored.

He growled up, "Do you have a **ladder?**"

Rapunzel

tossed

out

pancake

batter.

It covered him from head to toe.
She yelled, "It's better cooked, you know."

At this the poor prince had a cry,
then cupped his hands for one last try:

"Rapunzel, Rapunzel,
let down your BRAID!"

Confused

Rapunzel

pushed

out

her

maid.

The maid fell squarely on the prince,
quite pleased with the coincidence.

She nimbly jumped up off his lap
and soon revived the flattened chap.

Then smiling said, "For what it's worth,
you'll find I'm really down to earth."

His young heart thrilled, he gave a hoot,
for what was more, the maid was cute!

She set the prince upon his steed,
then leapt behind with graceful speed.

And leaning close so he could hear,
she whispered something in his ear:

"I fell for you when we first met."
He nodded. "How could I forget?"

Rapunzel watched them ride from sight.
"I'm glad I finally heard him right!

"I hope if they come back for more,
they'll think to knock on my back door."

For my own Prince Charming, who didn't give up on the first try.
With special thanks to Janice Graham and Rick Walton.   –L.W.

To Susan, Cecilia, Hilary and Frazer for all their support.   –L.M.

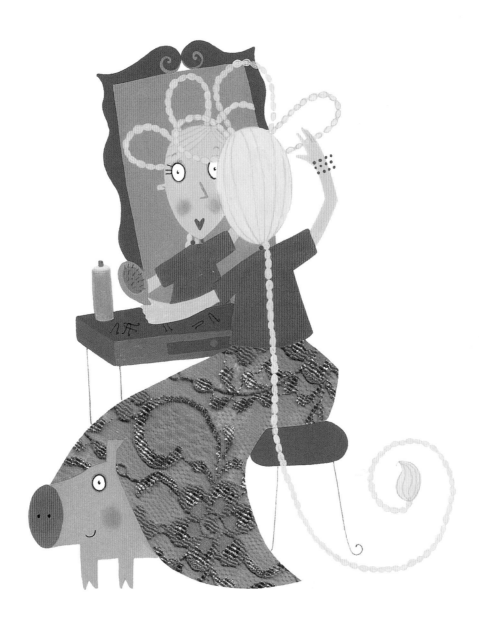

Published simultaneously in Canada. Manufactured in China
Designed by Gina DiMassi. Text set in Heatwave. The art was done in acrylic paint, paper montage, and colored pencils.
Library of Congress Cataloging-in-Publication Data   Wilcox, Leah. Falling for Rapunzel / Leah Wilcox ; illustrated by Lydia Monks.   p. cm.
Summary: A prince tries to get Rapunzel to throw down her hair so he can rescue her, but she mishears him and throws down
random objects from her room instead.   [1. Characters in literature–Fiction. 2. Humorous stories. 3. Stories in rhyme.]
I. Monks, Lydia, ill. II. Title. PZ8.3.W6587 Fal 2003 [E]–dc21 2001008521
ISBN 978-0-399-23794-2
13 15 17 19 20 18 16 14 12